D0426599

SAMANTHA AND THE MISSING PEARLS

SAMANTHA · 1904

BY VALERIE TRIPP

ILLUSTRATIONS DAN ANDREASEN

VIGNETTES SUSAN MCALILEY

THE AMERICAN GIRLS COLLECTION®

Published by Pleasant Company Publications
Previously published in *American Girl*® magazine
© Copyright 2001 by Pleasant Company
For information, address: Book Editor, Pleasant Company Publications,
8400 Fairway Place, P.O. Box 620998, Middleton, WI 53562.

Printed in Singapore.
01 02 03 04 05 06 07 08 TWP 10 9 8 7 6 5 4 3 2 1

Edited by Nancy Holyoke and Michelle Jones
Designed by Joshua Mjaanes and Laura Moberly
Art Directed by Joshua Mjaanes

Library of Congress Cataloging-in-Publication Data

Tripp, Valerie, 1951-
Samantha and the missing pearls / by Valerie Tripp ;
illustrations, Dan Andreasen ; vignettes, Susan McAliley.
p. cm. — (The American girls collection)
Summary: When her friend Nellie is suspected of stealing
Mrs. Van Sicklen's black pearls at Christmastime, Samantha helps her
discover where they really went.

ISBN 1-58485-275-5
[1. Christmas—Fiction. 2. Mystery and detective stories.]
I. Andreasen, Dan, ill. II. McAliley, Susan, ill. III. Title. IV. Series.
PZ7.T7363 Saj 2001   [Fic]—dc21   00-032652

The
AMERICAN GIRLS
COLLECTION
®

TABLE OF CONTENTS

SAMANTHA'S FAMILY

GRANDMARY
*Samantha's grandmother,
who wants her to be
a young lady.*

UNCLE GARD
*Samantha's favorite uncle,
who calls her Sam.*

SAMANTHA
*A nine-year-old orphan
who lives with her wealthy
grandmother.*

CORNELIA
*An old-fashioned beauty who
has newfangled ideas.*

NELLIE
*Samantha's friend
who works as a maid.*

MRS. VAN SICKLEN
*Grandmary's neighbor
and Nellie's boss.*

SAMANTHA AND THE MISSING PEARLS

R un, Samantha, run!" cried Nellie. "The dog is right behind us!"

Hearts pounding, Samantha and Nellie dashed across the drive and up the steps to Mrs. Van Sicklen's back porch. They flung open the kitchen door and ran inside. Nellie slammed the door shut, making the Christmas wreath swing wildly. Outside they heard noisy barking and the clumsy scrabbling of huge paws on the wooden porch floor.

Samantha leaned against the door and gasped, "I hate that dog."

"Me, too," agreed Nellie. "He's just as mean as his owner, Jones."

Jones was the new hired man at Mrs. Van Sicklen's house. Nellie and her family also worked for the Van Sicklens, and Jones had a room in the carriage house next to theirs. Jones was not a friendly neighbor. He never smiled and hardly ever spoke except to growl, "Stay away from there!" or "Watch out for that!" Jones was a handyman. He also emptied the ash cans, so he was always covered with gray ash.

"Jones is as gray as a ghost," said Samantha.

"He's an old crosspatch," said Nellie. "Yesterday he scolded me for cutting holly branches. I needed them to make wreaths."

"Oh, Nellie!" said Samantha. "Can you teach me to make a wreath?"

"Not right now," Nellie answered. "Mrs. Van Sicklen is having a tea party today, and I have to get everything ready. My mother and father are away."

"I'll help!" said Samantha. "I love tea parties. Who's coming?"

"Mrs. Eddleton and Mrs. Ryland," said Nellie.

Samantha made a face. "Oh dear me! How perfectly dreadful!" she said, imitating Mrs. Eddleton's shrill voice.

Mrs. Eddleton and Mrs. Ryland were hoity-toity ladies. They did not think Samantha and Nellie should be friends because Nellie was a servant and Samantha was a young lady.

Nellie grinned at Samantha's imitation, then turned to fill the kettle. "The ladies are going to give each other their Christmas presents," she said. "Mrs. Van Sicklen already opened the present her mother sent. You should see it, Samantha. It's a necklace of pearls. They're called black pearls, but they're really gray, a lovely dark—"

Suddenly the girls heard a shout. "Nellie!" It was Mrs. Van Sicklen.

"Nellie! Come quickly!" she cried.

4

Samantha and Nellie ran from the kitchen to the hallway and saw Mrs. Van Sicklen flying down the stairs. "They're gone!" she wailed. "My new black pearls! They've disappeared!"

"Oh, no!" gasped the girls.

Mrs. Van Sicklen's voice was shaky. "Those pearls are priceless!" she said.

"Mrs. Van Sicklen, ma'am, where did you last see the pearls?" Nellie asked.

"I put them on my dressing table last night," Mrs. Van Sicklen answered. "I've been in bed all day with a sick headache, so I didn't notice they were gone until just now. I was going to put them on to show the ladies at tea. But I've searched everywhere in my room, and they're gone!"

Before Nellie or Samantha could say another word, the doorbell rang. Nellie opened the door and there stood Mrs. Ryland and Mrs. Eddleton, their arms full of Christmas packages. When the ladies saw Mrs. Van Sicklen's face they both asked, "What's wrong?"

"You look so distressed, my dear!" said Mrs. Eddleton.

"My new black pearl necklace has disappeared!" said Mrs. Van Sicklen.

"You've been robbed! Call the police!" boomed Mrs. Ryland. She clutched her packages and looked all around as if the thief might be lurking nearby.

"Robbed! Oh dear me! How perfectly dreadful!" shrilled Mrs. Eddleton. She took Mrs. Van Sicklen by the elbow and led her toward the parlor.

"Do you really think . . ." Mrs. Van Sicklen began.

Mrs. Eddleton lowered her voice, but Samantha and Nellie both heard her say, "Of course! Didn't I tell you there'd be trouble when you hired that Nellie and her family to be servants?"

"But they were gone last night," said Mrs. Van Sicklen. "Well, all but Nellie."

"Nellie!" Mrs. Eddleton said as the parlor door closed behind her. "I never did trust that girl."

Samantha and Nellie looked at each other, horrified. "Oh, Nellie!" exclaimed Samantha. "They think *you* might have stolen the pearls! How dare they jump to that conclusion!"

Nellie's face was serious. "Samantha," she said quietly, "we've got to find those missing pearls. We've just got to."

"We will!" said Samantha firmly. "Let's go search Mrs. Van Sicklen's room.

Maybe she didn't look carefully enough."

Nellie led the way up the stairs and into Mrs. Van Sicklen's room. "When I came in this morning, Mrs. Van Sicklen was asleep," she explained. "I set her breakfast tray on the dressing table as usual. Then I swept the ashes from the fireplace into my ash scuttle, put coal on the grate, started a new fire, and took the ashes down to the cellar."

"Did you see the pearls on the dressing table?" asked Samantha.

"No," said Nellie, "but the room was dark. Let's search now."

The two girls searched through the powder puffs and perfume bottles, hairbrushes, hand mirrors, hankies, and hairpins on the dressing table. No pearls.

They crawled on their hands and knees to examine every inch of the floor. They wiggled under the bed, raked through the ashes in the fireplace, and even looked under the rug. No pearls.

"A thief must have come in last night when Mrs. Van Sicklen was asleep and stolen them," said Nellie.

"He probably planned this robbery very carefully," said Samantha.

"I don't think so," said Nellie. "Mrs. Van Sicklen got the necklace yesterday. No one saw it except me and . . ." Nellie stopped.

"Who?" asked Samantha.

"Jones!" said Nellie. "He was in the parlor fixing a chair when I brought Mrs. Van Sicklen the package. He saw her open it and take out the necklace."

"Jones!" exclaimed Samantha. "I bet *he* stole the pearls! Let's go search his room!"

"Oh, no, Samantha!" said Nellie. "I wouldn't dare! Besides, if Jones *did* steal the pearls, how did he get into the house last night? He doesn't have a key. And all the doors and windows are locked up tight."

"He could have broken a window to climb in," said Samantha. "Let's go search the outside of the house."

Samantha and Nellie crept down the stairs and past the parlor where the ladies were waiting for the police. Quickly, the girls put on their coats, peeked out the back door to be sure Jones was not around, and ran down the back steps. Just as they were coming around the corner of the house, Samantha saw Jones and his dog coming toward them across the drive. Instantly, Samantha drew back and held out her arm to stop Nellie until Jones and the dog had passed.

"Phew!" whispered Nellie in relief. "That was close!"

"Yes," said Samantha. "If Jones sees us searching the house, he may guess that we suspect him! Then he might do anything to stop us from proving he's the thief!"

The late December afternoon was

*Samantha drew back and held out her arm to stop
Nellie until Jones and the dog had passed.*

13

gloomy and raw. Samantha and Nellie searched every window and door for signs that someone had broken into the house, but they didn't find anything.

"I can't see the windows on the second and third floors very well," said Samantha. "We'll have to get a ladder, so I can get a better look."

"A ladder?" Nellie asked, shivering. They were standing next to the coal chute, feeling cold and discouraged. "You're going to climb up and look at every single window?"

"Well, I can't figure out how else Jones could have broken in," said Samantha.

"Me, either," said Nellie with a sigh.

14

She slumped back against the coal chute.

"Wait!" exclaimed Samantha. "The coal chute! It's never locked. Maybe Jones slid down the *chute* into the house."

"It's too narrow," said Nellie. "Jones could never fit in it."

Samantha pulled open the small trapdoor over the coal chute. "Let's see," she began.

But at that moment, Nellie and Samantha heard the clanking sound of the dog's collar. Both girls froze. Fear seemed to have fastened their feet to the ground.

"The dog," whispered Nellie, "and Jones! They're coming!"

"Quick!" said Samantha. "Hide!"

"But where?" asked Nellie.

Samantha looked around desperately. "Jump down the coal chute," she said.

"But . . ." Nellie protested.

"Go!" said Samantha, just as Jones and the dog rounded the corner and saw them. "Now!"

"Get away from there, you girls!" Jones yelled at them. But Nellie was already headed down the chute, with Samantha right behind her!

Swoosh! They slid down the short, steep chute. *Thud!* They landed on a pile of coal, making it spill out of the bin. The two girls rolled and tumbled to the cellar floor. Then *crash!* Their waving arms

Swoosh! They slid down the short, steep chute. Thud!
They landed on a pile of coal, making it spill out of the bin.

17

and legs knocked over ash cans that were filled to the brim. Ashes flew through the air like gray snow. The girls were coughing and choking when suddenly the cellar door swung open and all three ladies came thundering down the stairs.

"Good heavens!" gasped Mrs. Van Sicklen when she saw the girls sitting in the ashes. "What is going on here?"

Jones's gruff voice came from above, echoing down the coal chute. "They went and jumped down the chute, ma'am!" he announced. "Of all the fool things! Why, someone ought to . . ."

"That's enough, Jones!" said Mrs. Van Sicklen. They heard Jones slam shut the door to the chute with an angry *bang*.

"Girls," said Mrs. Van Sicklen. "How did you make this terrible mess?"

"Well," said Samantha. "Jones is right. We *did* jump down the coal chute."

"But *why?*" asked Mrs. Van Sicklen.

"We didn't mean any harm," said Samantha, glancing at Nellie as she struggled to her feet. Nellie didn't seem

19

to be paying any attention. Instead she was looking intently at something in the ashes by her skirt. Samantha went on, "We were trying to find your necklace and—"

But Nellie interrupted her. "And we *did* find it!" she said triumphantly.

Samantha gasped. There in Nellie's sooty hand was the necklace. It was covered with ashes, but it was not broken. "Oh, Nellie!" exclaimed Samantha. She gave her friend a hug. Then Nellie handed the necklace to Mrs. Van Sicklen.

"Thank you, Nellie," said Mrs. Van Sicklen. She looked relieved but confused.

"*How* did my necklace get down *here*?" she asked.

"It must have fallen off your dressing table," said Nellie. "I must have swept it up when I cleaned out your fireplace this morning. I guess I didn't notice it because the pearls are as gray as the ashes. I scooped the ashes and the necklace into the scuttle, carried them down here, and poured them into the ash can. Then when Samantha and I knocked over the cans, the necklace fell out. I found it in the ashes when I tried to stand up."

"But," fussed Mrs. Ryland, "what were you doing near the coal chute in the first place, and why did you jump down it?"

Samantha and Nellie looked at each other, shamefaced. "We were searching the house because we suspected Jo—I mean, we suspected a thief had broken in," said Samantha.

"You were not the only ones to suspect someone wrongly," said Mrs. Van Sicklen with a cool glance toward Mrs. Eddleton. "I'm proud of you girls and how you solved the mystery of my missing pearls. I can't imagine how you ever came to such a clever conclusion!"

"Well," said Samantha, grinning at Nellie, "you might say we *jumped* to that conclusion. But I don't think we'll jump to any more conclusions ever again. Do you, Nellie?"

"No," said Nellie, smiling. "Never again!"

VALERIE TRIPP

At 9   Now

My sisters and I loved to read the Nancy Drew mystery books. I think we read every single one. We admired Nancy because she was so brave and so clever. But I didn't want to grow up to be a detective. I wanted to write mystery stories. That's why writing this Samantha mystery was so much fun for me.

Valerie Tripp has written thirty-six books in The American Girls Collection, including six about Samantha.

Looking Back 1904

A PEEK INTO THE PAST

When Samantha was growing up in the early 1900s, Gertrude Chandler Warner, the creator of the Boxcar Children mystery series, was also growing up. Gertrude was born in 1890, and she lived right

Gertrude (upper left), age 11, with Frances, John, and her parents

across the street from a railroad station.

From the time Gertrude was five years old, she wanted to become an author. When Gertrude was nine years old, she and her sister, Frances, wrote and illustrated their

first book. It was called *Golliwogg at the Zoo*,
and they gave it to their grandfather for
Christmas. Every year after that, Gertrude
and her sister gave their grandparents a
new book. They called their publishing
company Warner & Co.

Gertrude also loved to read, and she
often went to the public library to find
books. Her favorite was *Alice's Adventures
in Wonderland*. One Saturday morning,
Gertrude checked out a book, read it, and

returned it that same day. But she was disappointed when she couldn't take another book out on the same day—she had to wait until Wednesday, the next time the library opened!

Another pastime Gertrude enjoyed was making furniture for her dollhouse. In 1916 she turned this childhood love

into her first published book, called *The House of Delight*. It was about her childhood dollhouse, where the china dolls Mr. and Mrs. Delight lived.

Gertrude began teaching in 1918, but she kept writing stories. One day, Gertrude

thought about another childhood memory.
She had always loved the excitement of
watching the freight trains speed past her
house. But what fascinated her the most
was the caboose at the end of each train.
Through the window of each caboose,
Gertrude could see a wooden table and a
small stove with a coffeepot. Sometimes
she could see men sitting at the table eat-
ing by the light of a lantern. Gertrude
always thought it would be fun to keep
house in a caboose.

She turned that memory into a story

about four children—Henry, Jessie, Violet, and Benny Alden—who lived in an old boxcar. The story was called *The Boxcar Children*.

Gertrude published the story in 1942. A few years later, she wrote *Surprise Island*, the second Boxcar book. In this story, the children solve a mystery, just as they do in the Boxcar books that followed. Gertrude wrote 19 Boxcar mysteries in all.

Gertrude's favorite place to write was her workroom at home. It

The Boxcar Children

had an easy chair
and wallpaper with
her favorite flower—
the violet. Gertrude
wrote her stories
by hand in blank
books. First she
wrote on the right-hand
pages, then she turned the book upside
down and wrote on the blank pages.
She wrote most of her stories four times
before they were just right.

The Boxcar Children books were
some of the first mysteries for children.
Gertrude loved thinking of new mysteries. She once said, "I would like to have
done what they did. I'd still like to do it."

"SHERLOCK HOLMES WELCOMED HER"

UNCOVER A MYSTERY!

Gather your friends and solve some mysteries.

When Samantha was a girl, there weren't many mystery stories written for children. Today, you can read mystery stories about children from all different time periods.

Invite your friends over for a Mystery Night. They can read some of the mysteries listed on the next page. Just make sure everybody reads the same ones! Then play games from Samantha's time to act out the stories.

Suspenseful Stories
Look for these stories in your local library.

The Secret of Gumbo Grove
BY ELEANORA E. TATE

Court of the Stone Children
BY ELEANOR CAMERON

Westminster West
BY JESSIE HAAS

The House of Dies Drear
BY VIRGINIA HAMILTON

Alice Rose & Sam
BY KATHRYN LASKY

Spying on Miss Müller
BY EVE BUNTING

Gaps in Stone Walls
BY JOHN NEUFELD

Also try these series:

The Boxcar Children

Nancy Drew Mystery Stories

Trixie Belden Mysteries

History Mysteries

The Adventures of Sherlock Holmes

Mandie Shaw

The Bobbsey Twins

Tableaux Vivants

Tableaux vivants (TAB-loh vee-VAHN) means "living pictures" in French. It was

The Boxcar Children

a popular game in Samantha's time. Divide into two teams. Team A poses as a scene from one of the books, using props if necessary. Team B tries to guess the scene. When Team B guesses correctly, the teams switch places.

Twenty Questions

One player thinks of a person, place, or thing from one of the books. The other players ask her yes-or-no questions to try to guess what she is thinking about. The players may not ask more than 20 questions. The first player to guess the answer gets to think of the next person, place, or thing. If no one guesses the answer, the first player goes again.

Assumed Characters

Divide into two teams, and silently act out a scene while the other team guesses what scene it is and what book it came from.

BUSINESS REPLY MAIL

FIRST-CLASS MAIL   PERMIT NO. 1137   MIDDLETON WI

POSTAGE WILL BE PAID BY ADDRESSEE

PO BOX 620497
MIDDLETON WI 53562-9940

American Girl®

Catalogue Request

Add your name and the name of a friend to our mailing list!
Simply fill in the names and addresses below and drop this
postage-paid card in the mail, visit our Web site at
www.americangirl.com, or call **1-800-845-0005.**

Send me a catalogue: **Send my friend a catalogue:**

My name _____   My friend's name _____

Address _____   Address _____

City _____ State _____ Zip 1961i   City _____ State _____ Zip 1225i

My e-mail address _____

My birth date: _____/_____/_____
              month day year

_____
Parent's signature